PUBLISHING

ISBN : 978-1-893951-54-9

10 9 8 7 6 5 4 3 2

Design: Dynamo Limited
Text: Kay Wilkins
Interior Artwork: Ailin Chambers

For information regarding permission,
write to VP Intellectual Property, Ripley Entertainment Inc.,
Suite 188, 7576 Kingspointe Parkway, Orlando, Florida 32819

Email: publishing@ripleys.com
www.ripleysrbi.com

Manufactured in Dallas, PA, United States
in May/2010 by Offset Paperback Manufacturers

2nd printing

———

Collector card picture credits: t/l ©francois brisson\fotolia.com; t/r Rinspeed;
b/l Dan Burton www.underwaterimages.co.uk

RIPLEY'S
RBI
FACT OR FICTION?
BUREAU of
INVESTIGATION

SECRETS OF THE DEEP

RIPLEY
PUBLISHING

a Jim Pattison Company

INTRODUCING THE RBI

Hidden away on a small island off the East Coast of the United States is Ripley High —a unique school for children who possess extraordinary talents.

Located in the former home of Robert Ripley—creator of the world-famous Ripley's Believe It or Not!—the school takes students who all share a secret. Although they look like you or me, they have amazing skills: the ability to conduct electricity, superhuman strength, or control over the weather—these are just a few of the talents the Ripley High School students possess.

The very best of these talented kids have been invited to join a top secret agency—Ripley's Bureau of Investigation: the RBI. This elite group operates from a hi-tech underground base hidden deep beneath the school. From here, the talented teen agents are sent on dangerous missions around the world, investigating sightings of fantastical creatures and strange occurrences. Join them on their incredible adventures as they seek out the weird and the wonderful, and try to separate fact from fiction ...

▶▶ RIPLEY

The Department of Unbelievable Lies

A mysterious rival agency determined to stop the RBI and discredit Ripley's by sabotaging the Ripley's database

The spirit of Robert Ripley lives on in RIPLEY, a supercomputer that stores the database—all Ripley's bizarre collections, and information on all the artifacts and amazing discoveries made by the RBI. Featuring a fully interactive holographic Ripley as its interface, RIPLEY gives the agents info on their missions and sends them invaluable data on their R-phones.

▶▶ Mr. Cain

The agents' favorite teacher, Mr. Cain, runs the RBI—under the guise of a Museum Club—and coordinates all the agents' missions.

▶▶ Dr. Maxwell

The only other teacher at the school who knows about the RBI. Dr. Maxwell equips the agents for their missions with cutting-edge gadgets from his lab.

MEET THE RBI TEAM

As well as having amazing talents, each of the seven members of the RBI has expert knowledge in their own individual fields of interest. All with different skills, the team supports each other at school and while out on missions, where the three most suitable agents are chosen for each case.

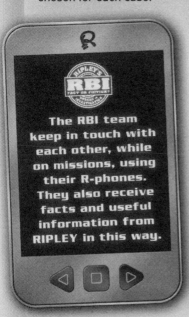

The RBI team keep in touch with each other, while on missions, using their R-phones. They also receive facts and useful information from RIPLEY in this way.

▶▶ KOBE

NAME : Kobe Shakur

AGE : 15

SKILLS : Excellent tracking and endurance skills, tribal knowledge, and telepathic abilities

NOTES : Kobe's parents grew up in different African tribes. Kobe has amazing tracking capabilities and is an expert on native cultures across the world. He can also tell the entire history of a person or object just by touching it.

▶▶ ZIA

NAME : Zia Mendoza

AGE : 13

SKILLS : Possesses magnetic and electrical powers. Can predict the weather

NOTES : The only survivor of a tropical storm that destroyed her village when she was a baby. Zia doesn't yet fully understand her abilities but she can predict and sometimes control the weather. Her presence can also affect electrical equipment.

▶▶ MAX

NAME : Max Johnson

AGE : 14

SKILLS : Computer genius and inventor

NOTES : Max, from Las Vegas, loves computer games and anything electrical. He spends most of his spare time inventing robots. Max hates school but he loves spending time helping Dr. Maxwell come up with new gadgets.

▶▶ KATE

NAME : Kate Jones

AGE : 14

SKILLS : Computer-like memory, extremely clever, and ability to master languages in minutes

NOTES : Raised at Oxford University in England, by her history professor and part-time archaeologist uncle, Kate memorized every book in the University library after reading them only once!

▶▶ ALEK

NAME : Alek Filipov

AGE : 15

SKILL : Contortionist with amazing physical strength

NOTES : Alek is a member of the Russian under-16 Olympic gymnastics team and loves sports and competitions. He is much bigger than the other agents, and although he seems quiet and serious much of the time, he has a wicked sense of humor.

▶▶ LI

NAME : Li Yong

AGE : 15

SKILL : Musical genius with pitch-perfect hearing and the ability to mimic any sound

NOTES : Li grew up in a wealthy family in Beijing, China, and joined Ripley High later than the other RBI agents. She has a highly developed sense of hearing and can imitate any sound she hears.

▶▶ JACK

NAME : Jack Stevens

AGE : 14

SKILLS : Can "talk" to animals and has expert survival skills

NOTES : Jack grew up on an animal park in the Australian outback. He has always shared a strong bond with animals and can communicate with any creature— and loves to eat weird food!

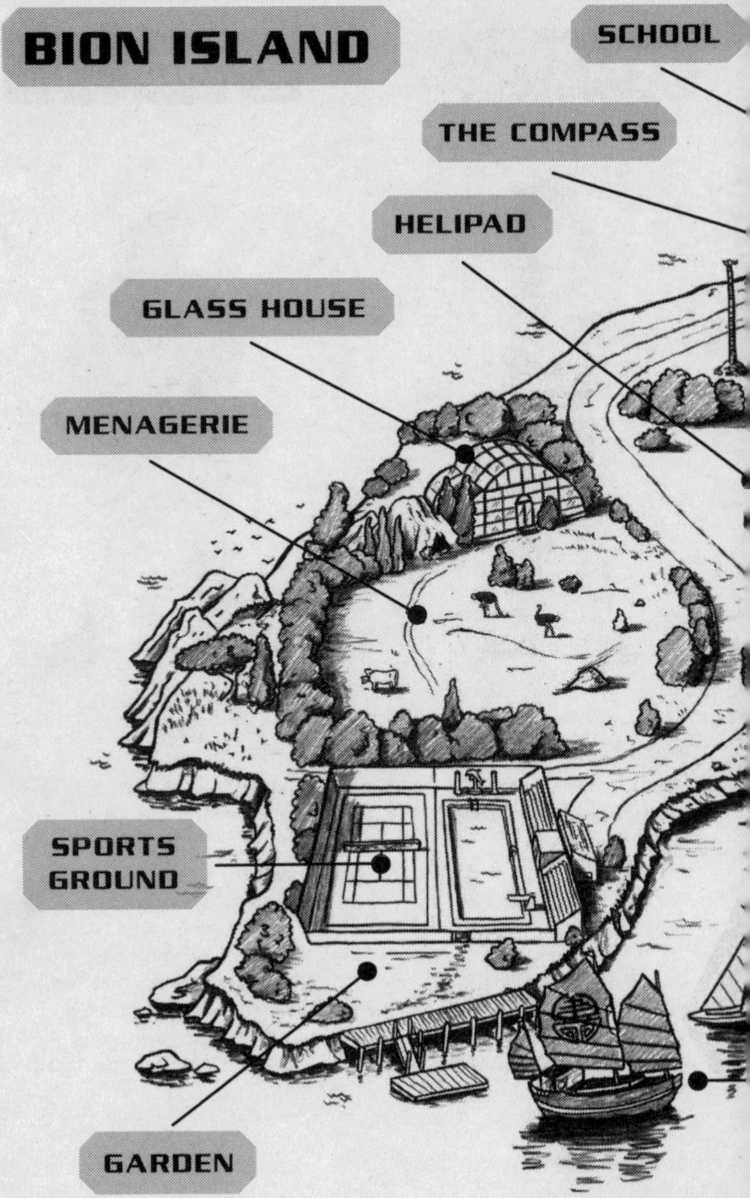

BION ISLAND

SCHOOL

THE COMPASS

HELIPAD

GLASS HOUSE

MENAGERIE

SPORTS GROUND

GARDEN

CHINESE GARDEN

STONE MONUMENT
(Secret Entrance)

WATER
ENTRANCE
TO SECRET
CAVE

SECRET RBI LAB

DOCKS

MON LEI

Prologue

This diving group had been really lucky. Not only had they managed to see a swordfish and a turtle, but a group of dolphins had played alongside them for almost five minutes.

As he led his group of happy tourists home, Minas noticed a large shape appear, casting a cool, gray shadow over the otherwise crystal-blue water. Minas had been a diving instructor long enough to know exactly what that particular shadow was—a very large shark.

Minas signaled that his group should follow him, hoping to move the inexperienced divers to safety before they noticed anything was wrong. But it was already too late. One by one they all saw the enormous, angry silver shape headed toward them.

Trying his best to stay calm, Minas saw a narrow fissure in one of the rocks and guided the group inside. Outside the shark prowled, but was too big to follow his prey in. Their hideaway led into a series of tunnels, which Minas thought could be another way out for his group. He led them as quickly and efficiently as he could through the network of darkness, until suddenly the tunnel gave way to a huge cavern.

Swimming into this enormous chamber, Minas's diver's light picked out shapes and textures in the gloom that took on an eerie green glow as the shimmering yellow beam hit them.

He swam farther into the cave, only to quickly jump back. A gnarled hand seemed to stretch up from the ocean floor, as if reaching for him to try to drag him down. Minas realized that the hand was not moving after all, but then saw it was not the only one. Ghostly limbs jutted out at strange angles from all over the seabed. Minas signaled for his dive group to stay where they were, this was no place for tourists. It seemed that they had stumbled on some sort of underwater graveyard, and looking at the way those bodies were reaching for help, it seemed to Minas that they were not resting peacefully.

Serious Swimming

"Now I'm beginning to get bored," complained Max.

The RBI boys had decided to have a swimming competition in the school pool. Max and Jack had both given up what felt like hours ago, but Alek and Kobe were still going strong, trying to beat each other.

"Mate, I've been bored for about half an hour now," said Jack with a sigh. Max looked down

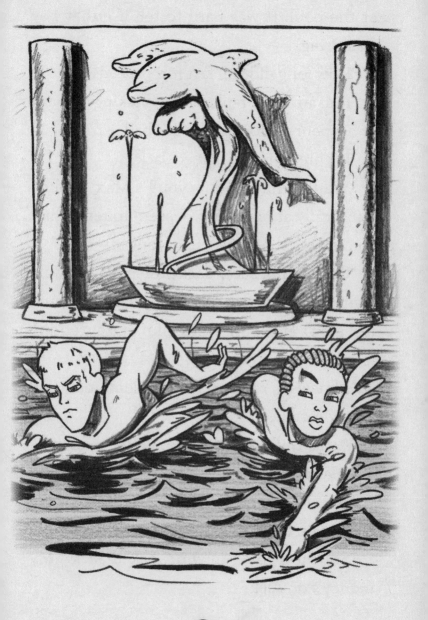

at the pool. It was hard to tell if either boy was tiring.

"How long did you last for?" asked Jack.

"Half an hour," replied Max, shaking his head at his poor performance. "It's bad, isn't it?"

"It's pretty poor," agreed Jack.

"Wait, what about you?" Max looked quizzically at his friend. "I seem to remember you hitting the showers not long after me."

"Um, I'm not sure," Jack pretended to think, trying not to answer the question, but he could feel Max's eyes boring into him. "Okay, I think it was 35 minutes."

"I knew it! You're no better than me," said Max gleefully.

"Actually, I'm five minutes better than you," said Jack.

Max smiled and looked back at their friends tearing up the pool trying to beat each other.

"So who's going to win?" asked Jack. "My money's on Alek."

"No way, man," Max shook his head. "Kobe, all the way. It's like he's specially programmed to never admit defeat."

"But I've seen Alek swim up and down that pool for the whole day," said Jack.

"Then we are in for a long wait!" said Max. "Because Kobe's never giving up. It's so amazing that he couldn't even swim when he came to Ripley High, but now he's a swimming star!"

Jack had to admit that Max had a point. Alek was, indeed, the superstar sportsman. His amazing strength was only matched by his sheer love of competition when it came to sports, but even Alek had his limits. Kobe, on the other hand, had none of Alek's power or skill

▶▶ Martin Strel swam the length of the Amazon River in South America in just 66 days. This is the equivalent of swimming 105,500 lengths of an Olympic swimming pool. Strel swam for ten hours a day and faced encounters with piranhas, sharks, and crocodiles.

when it came to sports such as swimming, but one of Kobe's abilities was endurance and the ability to pick up new skills. The tall, thin Kenyan was often overlooked for sports teams, but you could bet that he would always be the last one out on the basketball court, the football field, or in the swimming pool, long after everyone else had tired—and generally looking as if he could still go on for another few hours!

"Man, I'm hungry," Max complained, "and I have a feeling these two could go on swimming for days!"

Jack pulled a cereal bar out of his bag and handed it to Max. Max studied the label.

"Honey and oats?" he questioned. "That's a little normal for you, isn't it?" Jack smiled.

"What were you expecting it would be?"

"Cricket and cockroach maybe?" said Max. Jack playfully hit his friend on the shoulder. On missions in wild locations, Jack was only too happy to try some of the local flavors—

he often found bugs tastier than some of the food served in the Ripley High cafeteria! His fondness for "bush tucker" had earned him quite a reputation among his friends.

"I'll have it back, if you don't want it," Jack teased.

"Kobe's pulling ahead!" Max shouted, as he forced his mouth full of cereal bar. "Ko-be, Ko-be," he started cheering.

Jack smiled; it would be nice for Kobe to win. Alek usually won absolutely everything, and although years ago he'd given up trying to beat his Russian classmate, Jack knew that secretly Kobe still held on to the hope that maybe one day he might beat Alek. Perhaps this was the day. Besides, it would be fun to tease Alek about losing; it happened so rarely that Jack wasn't sure how his friend would react.

"Go, Kobe, go!" Max yelled beside him, as Kobe started to pull away.

Jack felt his jacket pocket vibrate. He pulled out his R-phone to see that he had a "Museum Club" message from Mr. Cain.

"Looks like they're going to have to settle this another day," he said.

"I don't know what you mean," said Max, reading his own Museum Club message. "I'd say Kobe won that."

2

The Lost City

"There was no winner," declared Alek, as the four boys walked into the secret RBI base. He was toweling his hair off where it was still wet from the pool. "I would have caught Kobe at the next change of ends and been back in the lead."

"So you admit, then, that Kobe was ahead?" asked Max.

"No, not ahead," said Alek, "just a little bit in front."

"Ahead, in front, it's all the same," argued Max.

"Not necessarily," Kate put in, overhearing their conversation. "If you look at the definitions for, and origins of, the two words, you'll find that—"

"Thank you," said Max, cutting her off quickly. "I really don't need to know."

"I was just trying to help," said Kate, looking slightly put out.

"And you did," Alek told her, as he pulled out one of the RBI base's strange, futuristic-looking chairs next to Kate. "You helped prove that there was no winner, and that I didn't lose."

"What do you think, Kobe?" asked Zia, who was perched on a table near Kate and Alek. Kobe shrugged.

"It doesn't really make much difference," he said. Then a cheeky glint appeared in his eye. "But I know that I won."

"Yeah!" said Max, as he gave Kobe a high-five.

"Oh good, you're all here," said Mr. Cain, as he walked into the room.

"We've been here for ages," said Max, pushing the sunglasses he always wore back up onto the top of his head.

"I was just trying to check some last minute details on this mission," said Mr. Cain.

"What is it that you were trying to find out, Sir?" asked Zia.

"The location, actually," Mr. Cain told them with a smile. The RBI agents all looked at each other, puzzled. How could they be briefed on a mission if there was no location?

At that moment, RIPLEY appeared. The holographic head of Robert Ripley looked around at the agents in front of him and then turned to Mr. Cain.

"Any luck?" he asked.

Mr. Cain shook his head. "We're no clearer on

an exact location and have no video footage."

"Video footage of what?" asked Jack.

"Of the subject of your mission," said Mr. Cain. "RIPLEY, you might as well brief them."

"There have been reports that a diving instructor in Greece was coming to the end of a session with some tourists when, believe it or not, he stumbled upon what he described as an underwater graveyard." Ripley told the agents.

"Why would they bury anyone underwater?" asked Kobe.

"I don't think they did," said RIPLEY. "The way he described arms reaching up toward him and legs sticking out at uncomfortable angles, it doesn't sound like this is any sort of restful burial ground."

"Do you mean they could come back as zombies?" asked Max, sounding slightly hopeful.

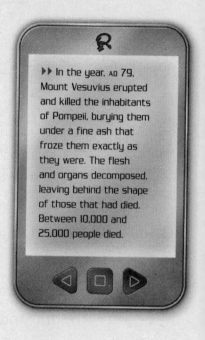

>> In the year, AD 79, Mount Vesuvius erupted and killed the inhabitants of Pompeii, burying them under a fine ash that froze them exactly as they were. The flesh and organs decomposed, leaving behind the shape of those that had died. Between 10,000 and 25,000 people died.

"Don't be silly," Kate scolded him.

"It will be the result of some sort of natural disaster," Zia offered quietly, "an earthquake, or a volcanic eruption."

"Like in Pompeii," said Kate. "People there were frozen exactly as they were when the volcano erupted. It's spooky."

"But how did the people get underwater in the first place?" asked Max.

"It will be the ruins of a city and whatever natural disaster killed those people will have also pushed the whole city into the sea," said Kate.

"Oh," said Max, sounding slightly disappointed.

"Do you think it could be an underwater city?" Kate asked Ripley, excitement edging into her voice. "Do you know which one it is?"

"Unfortunately not," said the hologram. "The diver was trying to escape from a particularly angry shark when he and his tour group found the ruins, and he hasn't been able to locate them again."

"But it's real?" asked Li. "It's not just someone making up a horror story about people who died long ago underwater trying to claim their next victims?"

Jack looked at her quizzically.

"Sorry, I saw a film like that once," she explained. "It was really scary! But somebody could be trying to confuse us, or—"

"Or trying to get a lie into the database," finished Jack.

"Like DUL," said Max. The Department of Unbelievable Lies, or DUL, was always trying to disrupt all the hard work that the RBI did.

"We thought that at first, too," said Mr. Cain. "But there are 15 people in the diving group who all back up our diving guide's story."

"So this is a real, undiscovered, underwater city?" asked Kate, her eyes wide with excitement.

"It looks that way," said Mr. Cain.

Kate jumped up from her seat. "It could be the lost city of Atlantis! Do you realize what this discovery could mean?"

"I've never heard of Atlantis," said Max. "Where is it?"

"No one knows," Kate almost snapped. She was trying very hard to keep the frustration out of her voice. "That's why it's lost."

"There is a legend that a long time ago, there

was an island that sunk into the sea." Li, stepped in before Kate and Max got into an argument.

"An island that was home to a really advanced group of people," added Kate. "They had technology that we still haven't discovered today."

"Oh, yeah," Max seemed to be remembering something. "I've heard that story. It's about aliens, isn't it?"

"No, it's not about aliens, you—"

"Anyway," Mr. Cain interrupted, before Kate could call Max whatever name she was about to. "To answer your question, Kate, yes, it could well be Atlantis, but even if it isn't, it is a very exciting find, and to answer your next question before you even ask it, yes, you can be on the investigating team."

"It's going to be amazing!" said Kate.

"Unless, of course Li was right," said Max. "And what you are going to investigate is, in fact, a city of the un-dead who want to drag you down into their watery graves."

"I was joking," said Li. "I don't think they're really ghosts or zombies."

"Good," said Mr. Cain. "Because you're going to be on the team too."

Max smiled as he noticed Li looked just a

little worried that she might come face to face with a ghost.

"Alek, you'll be the third agent," said Mr. Cain. "I think your ability to hold your breath for so long and your swimming skills might be useful here."

"That's funny," said Jack. "I'd heard it was Kobe who was the best at swimming."

"Did you mean to say Alek was going for his zombie-fighting abilities?" asked Max.

Li turned slightly pale as she pretended not to be worried.

3

Power Packs and Pyramids

"So you're off to discover the lost city, are you?" asked Dr. Maxwell, as the agents chosen for the mission walked into his lab.

Alek wondered how Dr. Maxwell always knew all the details of their missions before they had even told him. Especially this mission, when Mr. Cain only just seemed to have worked the plan out himself!

"We're hoping it's Atlantis," Li told Dr.

Maxwell excitedly, "and that the bodies really are dead."

"Well, Atlantis really would be something exciting." Dr. Maxwell looked a bit confused at Li's last comment. "So you'll be needing some exciting gadgets to take with you." He opened a cupboard and began pulling things out. He placed on the table what looked to Kate like some sort of mask.

"What are those?" she asked.

"They are the latest in CCUBA equipment," he told her. "It stands for closed circuit underwater breathing apparatus—CCUBA! The air is recycled through your face masks, filtering out the carbon dioxide."

"Is that why the mask covers our mouths too?" asked Li.

"Aha, you spotted that," said Dr. Maxwell. "No, that is so you can talk underwater." The agents looked at each other, slightly confused. "A small micro-transmitter is hidden in the face mask and will carry sound from one to the other."

"That's amazing," said Li, as she examined one of the masks, looking for the tiny radio. "It's so small and light. So all we need are these masks?"

"Pretty much. The super-advanced CCUBA system it uses means that the air tanks are tiny. It's a good thing too, or it wouldn't leave room for this." Dr. Maxwell lifted his next piece of equipment into view. It looked like a jetpack. "This is the PPP."

"Is this one of Max's inventions so he can look like a superhero?" Alek asked. Dr. Maxwell laughed.

"No, it's a very real, professionally-made, personal propulsion pack." He picked it up and helped Alek to strap the PPP onto his back. At the bottom, where a jetpack's thrusters would be, there was a large propeller that pointed toward the floor.

"I feel like a rocket man," said Alek, a huge smile on his face as he imagined Max's envy. Dr. Maxwell reached over and pressed the power button and at once the propeller kicked into action. Alek felt himself struggling to stay still as the air hit the floor around him, trying to push him upward. Kate and Li giggled as he danced from foot to foot, trying to keep his balance.

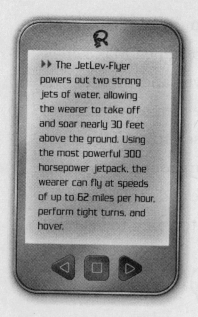

▶▶ The JetLev-Flyer powers out two strong jets of water, allowing the wearer to take off and soar nearly 30 feet above the ground. Using the most powerful 300 horsepower jetpack, the wearer can fly at speeds of up to 62 miles per hour, perform tight turns, and hover.

Dr. Maxwell turned the PPP off again.

"It's so powerful," said Alek.

"I don't think I would have stayed standing." Li was looking suspiciously at the propeller pack.

"No, I'm not sure you would have," said Dr. Maxwell. "The PPP is a wonderful piece of equipment. It's made of really lightweight material, but its size and power might not be so good for smaller agents."

Li smiled, realizing Dr. Maxwell was talking about her.

"But that's not the end of the world," he said. "I have something else for you two girls to try." He handed them each two small devices. "These are PPPPs—personal podiatric propulsion systems."

"Podiatric means 'of the feet'," said Kate.

"Exactly," Dr. Maxwell agreed. "These are propellers for your feet."

Li strapped on the PPPPs. "They're not very stylish," she complained.

"But they will help you move quickly should you be chased by any ghosts or zombies," Dr. Maxwell teased her.

Li's face went white. "Why do you say that?" she asked. "What have you heard?"

"I've heard that you have a very active imagination, and that Max likes to scare people," said Dr. Maxwell with a grin.

Li relaxed slightly, but gripped her propeller tightly, as if it might save her life.

Dr. Maxwell gave Alek a piece of paper with the number 24 on it.

"What's this?" he asked.

"It's the number of my space in the school parking lot," Dr. Maxwell explained. "Why don't you take my new car for a spin on this trip?"

"I'm not really sure this is going to be the best mission for that, Sir," said Alek looking at the number in his hand.

Dr. Maxwell raised an eyebrow. "You'd be surprised," he said.

"Hello, Miss Burrows," Li and Kate chimed together, as the three agents walked into their geography classroom.

"Ah, my two favorite pupils," said Miss Burrows. "Oh, and Alek," she added, seeing him come in behind the two enthusiastic girls. "Nice to see you taking an interest in geography. What can I do for the three of you?"

"We want to know about Atlantis," Kate told her teacher.

"Ooh, I love that story," said Miss Burrows. "What do you want to know?"

Kate and Li glanced at each other. Miss Burrows didn't know about the RBI; very few teachers in the school did, as it was top secret. They needed to come up with a cover story for their sudden interest in Atlantis.

"Alek was telling us that he thought he heard on the news that it had been discovered," said Kate. She knew that if there had been any news in the historical or geographical magazines about a lost city being discovered that Miss Burrows would probably be the person who would know about it.

"Well, I haven't heard that," said Miss Burrows. "Of course, Atlantis could just be a myth, as there has never been any proof that it existed." She switched on her laptop computer and began pulling files on to the desktop and opening them.

"There have been a few major discoveries in recent years," she told them. "Underwater relics and ruins that people have thought to be Atlantis." Miss Burrows pressed a button on her computer and started a slide show. She turned the computer toward the RBI agents and the screen filled with a blue image. Looking carefully at the picture, the agents could make out what looked like some stone steps, underwater.

"This image is from an underwater site discovered in 1985 near Yonaguni, Japan," Miss Burrows told them. "It is thought to be the remains of a pyramid that could be hundreds of years older than the Egyptian pyramids."

"Did they find any bodies there?" asked Alek.

"No, I don't think they did," said Miss Burrows. "Any bodies would have decayed into the earth centuries ago."

"What if they were cast in lava, like the people at Pompeii," asked Kate.

"Then I suppose they could still be there, but I'm fairly sure there were no bodies found at Yonaguni."

"Were there any stories of ghosts?" asked Li.

"No," said Miss Burrows, thinking carefully. "Although many of the ancient Egyptian burial sites have been thought to have curses attached to them. When Tutankhamun's tomb was discovered it was thought that anyone who disturbed it was cursed."

"But it was all just a myth, right?" asked Li hopefully.

"There were deaths linked to the discovery, but they could all be explained. Some people think that they were just coincidence, whereas

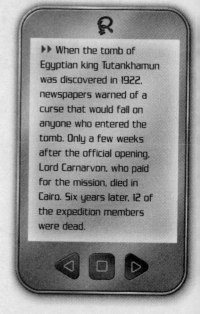

▶▶ When the tomb of Egyptian king Tutankhamun was discovered in 1922, newspapers warned of a curse that would fall on anyone who entered the tomb. Only a few weeks after the official opening, Lord Carnarvon, who paid for the mission, died in Cairo. Six years later, 12 of the expedition members were dead.

others claim to be able to argue that it was King Tut's curse."

"Oh," said Li, remembering the description of the hand reaching out toward the diver as if it wanted to pull him down.

"Thanks, Miss Burrows," said Kate pulling her nervous friend with her as they left the room. "There's no such thing as zombies, ghosts, or curses," she said.

Li, however, did not look so sure.

4

Jaws

Early the next morning, the three agents arrived at the school parking lot. They walked up and down the lines of teachers' cars, looking for the lot number Dr. Maxwell had given them.

"I bet he's got a really old-fashioned car," suggested Li. "Something geeky and beige."

"Beige?" Kate asked.

"Beige equals boring," Li explained.

"So you don't think Dr. Maxwell would

have something sleek, silver, and super cool?" asked Alek.

"No way!" said Li. "Dr. Maxwell's a great teacher, but super cool? I don't think so. I mean have you seen his hair?" Li suddenly realized that the others had stopped, and turned around to see why.

Kate and Alek were standing by a shiny, futuristic-looking, silver sports car.

"Ohmigosh! That is awesome!" cried Li, as she rushed over. "Whose car is that?"

The agents watched amazed as the driver's door opened upward. Dr. Maxwell stepped out and threw the keys to Kate.

"This is Jaws," he told them. "It's an amphibious vehicle."

"What does that mean?" asked Li.

"It means that Jaws works in water as well as on land," he explained. "On the water and under the water, in fact."

"Won't we be noticed driving a car underwater?" asked Kate.

"That's one of the wonderful things about Jaws," said Dr. Maxwell. "It's been specially designed so that at the touch of a button it can transform to be almost unnoticeable underwater."

"So why is it called Jaws?" asked Alek.

"I was hoping you'd ask that," said Dr. Maxwell. "I nicknamed the car Jaws because when it transforms it looks incredibly like a shark."

"A shark?" asked Alek.

"No one would question a large shark moving through the water," their teacher explained as he handed Li a map.

"Will this tell us how to get there?" she asked.

"Sort of," Dr. Maxwell said with a smile. "It's not exactly a road map, but it will give you the general direction. It's fairly easy, though. From here you go around Long Island until you reach the Ocean Landmark and then it's across the Atlantic all the way to the Strait of Gibraltar. Once you're in the Mediterranean, it's plain sailing, just

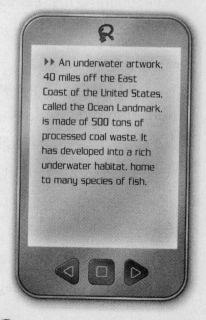

▶▶ An underwater artwork, 40 miles off the East Coast of the United States, called the Ocean Landmark, is made of 500 tons of processed coal waste. It has developed into a rich underwater habitat, home to many species of fish.

follow the African coastline."

It didn't really sound like "plain sailing" to Li, but she hoped that the map would explain everything. She jumped into the back of the car and opened the map on her lap.

"Hey, why do you get to drive?" Alek asked Kate, as she swung into the driver's seat.

"Because Dr. Maxwell gave me the keys," she told him. "We'll swap halfway if you like."

"Great, then I can sleep for the first part," said Alek, pushing his seat back as far as it would go. Li quickly pulled her legs up and moved farther behind Kate.

"I wonder if there are any dark glasses in here that would block out the light and help me sleep," Alek said, as he rummaged through the glove compartment. Instead, he pulled out a pair of binoculars. "Hey, what are these?" he asked. "They look like night-vision goggles."

"That's exactly what they are," said Dr. Maxwell, as he leaned into the passenger window. "I have things in there for every possible event." He turned to Li. "I've even got a mirror in there if you need to use one," he said smiling. "You know it takes a lot of effort to get my hair to look this good."

As Dr. Maxwell ran a hand through his wild, bushy brown hair, Li blushed with embarrassment, realizing that her voice must have traveled in the underground parking lot and the professor had heard her earlier comment.

Kate drove the car around the island to the dock. She paused as they reached the water's edge.

"This car definitely goes underwater?" she asked.

"That's what Dr. Maxwell said," Alek told her.

"Alright, here we go."

Kate drove the car forward again and plunged Jaws into the water. As she did, the silver car's underwater technology kicked in and it began to transform, just as Dr. Maxwell said it would. First, the wing mirrors folded in flat against the sides of the car. Then the wheel arches extended down, covering the wheels, to become pectoral fins at the front and pelvic fins at the back. The rear spoiler began to whir as it unfolded and extended into a tail shape. The roof lowered a fraction as a submarine-style periscope appeared in the center, disguising itself as a dorsal fin, and the whole car adjusted slightly, becoming longer and thinner to help add to the shark-like appearance.

Li shuffled into the middle of the back seat as the sides narrowed around her.

"Let's see how this shark really moves," said Kate, as she pushed the gas pedal to the floor.

Jaws roared as it sprang into life. Bubbles rushed along past the side windows as the car's nose dived deeper into the water.

"I thought we'd slow down in water," said Alek. "But I think we've actually speeded up.

"It's really an amazing feeling," said Kate. "The car just cuts through the water so easily."

"It's beautiful," said Li as she looked out of the back windows. "There are so many colors

this far under the water. The fish are moving out of our way, but they're still closer than I've ever seen them before."

"We do look like a shark to them," Kate reminded her.

"Remember not to open any windows!" Alek reminded the girls. "The cabin is watertight and we have air circulating in here, but as soon as we open the windows the seal will break and the sea would come rushing in."

"Good point," said Li, "but I'm quite happy to look at the fish on the other side of the glass."

Almost 12 hours later, Alek docked Jaws at the harbor in Crete and the agents made their way to the Poseidon Diving School. Minas Lamprakis, the instructor who had found the underwater graveyard, greeted them as they arrived.

"I am so sorry I can't remember more," he said, after telling them about the events that had led up to his discovery. "I was just so focused on getting my group back to safety that I didn't pay attention to where I was."

"It's okay," said Kate. "You know the basic area and we can search from there."

"Have you eaten?" Minas asked the agents.

"No and I'm starving," said Alek. "I found a packet of chips that Dr. Maxwell had left, but other than that I've not had anything since we left this morning."

"You only left this morning and you came by sea?" asked Minas. "That's incredibly fast."

"We drove," Li told him with a smile.

Minas took the agents to a little restaurant overlooking the sea, and they watched the sunset cast pink and purple shadows onto the aqua-green water.

"I remember a narrow opening in the rock that I pulled my

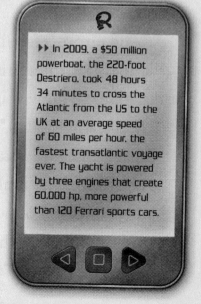

▶▶ In 2009, a $50 million powerboat, the 220-foot Destriero, took 48 hours 34 minutes to cross the Atlantic from the US to the UK at an average speed of 60 miles per hour, the fastest transatlantic voyage ever. The yacht is powered by three engines that create 60,000 hp, more powerful than 120 Ferrari sports cars.

group into," Minas told them, still desperately trying to remember something that might help. "We swam through some tunnels trying to find a way out, and then there were those ... hands."

Li felt a shiver pass through her body as Minas mentioned the hands.

"None of your dive party has been ill or anything since, have they?" she asked thinking about the idea of curses.

"No, not at all," Minas told her. "Why do you ask?"

"And no one's felt like they've been called to the sea, as if the spirits of the people trapped there were pulling you back?"

Minas smiled. "No," he told her reassuringly. "Those remains did scare me at first. They were so eerie and unnatural looking, as if the people had been carved out of the seabed itself." His eyes focused on the distance as he recalled the memory. "But now I'm not scared of them. I feel sorry for those people. Imagine your final resting place being hidden for so long, and especially after the horrible deaths they must have experienced."

Li nodded, but thought that was as good a reason as any for a spirit to become restless and turn into a ghost.

"You really don't need to worry, Li," said Alek, although his attention was focused on something out at sea. Small lights flashed in the black night, picking up the ripples on the now dark sea. Kate looked too and realized that there was something strange about seeing so few lights on such a dark night.

"What are they?" she asked. She could tell that Alek felt the same uneasiness that she did about the lights. Kate could think of no good reason for someone to be out on the sea at night with no lights on their boat.

"I'll be right back," said Alek, quickly getting up from the table.

"I'm not sure what they are," said Minas. "Those lights have been out there every night for over a week now. I just assumed that it was fishermen. The lights on their boat must have broken so they're using torches instead."

"Maybe they would have done that once, but it seems a little odd to go out night after night in a broken boat," said Kate.

"I think you're right," said Li. "The lights aren't bright enough for them to be able to find their way back. It could be dangerous for them."

"Especially if there are sharks out there," Kate added.

Alek reappeared, jogging toward them with something in his hand.

"Dr. Maxwell's night-vision goggles," he told the others, as he put them on. "It's definitely some sort of boat," he said. "Only I don't think they're fishing. It looks like they are trying to throw something into the water. What do you think?"

Alek passed the goggles to Kate so that she could see.

"It looks like something heavy," said Kate. "I can see them struggling with it." She passed the glasses to Li, who took a few steps forward off the terrace and away from the restaurant. Realizing what was happening, Alek and Kate followed. Out of the noise of the restaurant, Li's super-sensitive hearing would allow her to pick out more of what was happening.

"Whatever it is just went in," she told them. "I heard the splash. It didn't sound heavy enough to be metal, so it's not a treasure chest. It sounded almost fleshy, like the noise Alek makes when he dives into the pool."

Kate and Alek exchanged nervous glances.

"Do you mean it sounds like a body?" asked Kate.

"No, not quite." Li strained to make out the size of the splash. "Smaller than that. More like part of a body." She laughed, but then took a sharp breath as she realized what she had said. "You don't think it is part of a body, do you? It's not the curse is it?"

"I'm sure it's not," said Alek. "But I certainly think we've found somewhere to start our search tomorrow. We might just have a second mystery on our hands."

5

Shark Shocks

The following day, the RBI agents drove their underwater car to the place where they had seen the dark boat the night before.

"I just can't get used to the fact that we are now inside a shark," said Li as, once again, the rear of the car narrowed around her.

"It's pretty awesome," Alek agreed.

As the car dropped deeper into the ocean, Alek put the headlights on. Outside, it would now look as if the shark had glowing eyes.

"If we look like a shark, won't we attract more sharks?" asked Li. "What if another shark takes a fancy to us?"

"Dr. Maxwell thought of that," Kate said, reassuring her friend. "He fitted Jaws with anti-shark technology."

"How does that work?" asked Li.

"There are points around the car that give off a very small electrical current," Kate explained. "Sharks have special sensing organs that allow them to feel changes in the water, like if the temperature changes. Even a very low amount of electricity will overload these senses and make them feel a bit uncomfy."

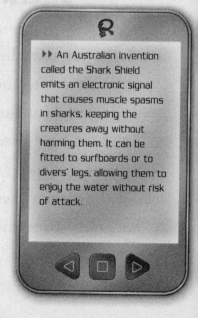

▶▶ An Australian invention called the Shark Shield emits an electronic signal that causes muscle spasms in sharks, keeping the creatures away without harming them. It can be fitted to surfboards or to divers' legs, allowing them to enjoy the water without risk of attack.

"A shark shock," said Alek.

"But it doesn't hurt the shark?" asked Li.

"No, the voltage is so low that it won't hurt the shark, or anything else in the sea," said Kate.

"I really can't see anything that looks strange or unusual around here," said Alek. "Are you sure this is the right place?"

"I memorized the location," said Kate. She was slightly put out that Alek was questioning her photographic memory.

"I know how good your memory is," said Alek. "I was just wondering if you might have taken a wrong turn somewhere."

"My driving is just as good as my memory!" said Kate.

"Why don't we leave the car here and try swimming?" suggested Li. "We might find something then."

Jaws rose to the surface of the water, still

disguised as a shark. Alek pressed a button that would anchor it in place. The RBI team then strapped on all the diving equipment that Dr. Maxwell had given them, and left the car.

"It just looks like a normal ocean floor," said Li, communicating with the other agents through the radio microphones in their specially adapted diving masks. "I can't see anything unusual at all."

"There must be," said Alek. "We all saw that boat drop something into the water."

They were very deep now, almost on the ocean floor. The light hardly reached this far below the surface and, even through their wetsuits, the water felt incredibly cold.

"Perhaps it was something that was alive ..." suggested Kate, feeling spooked by the shadows the ocean life was creating around her, "... like a turtle that could have swum away by now." A dark shape passed over the group, cutting off the little sunlight that had managed to break through. Kate shivered, and told herself that it was just a friendly dolphin.

Alek was beginning to get frustrated that their search had brought them nothing. "I just can't understand—" he started.

Li raised a hand indicating to Alek that she needed silence. "I can hear a noise," she said. "It sounds like something moving through the water."

As she tuned into the sound Li remembered her fear at the thought of the hands reaching up from their watery graves.

"No, make that *somethings*," said Li, "and they're moving fast! You don't think it's the bodies, do you?"

Li never got her answer. Kate felt something smooth and strong brush against her wetsuit. Terrified of what she might see, she slowly turned her diver's light toward the source of the bump and found herself face-to-face with a shark!

To her left, Li screamed. Kate turned quickly to see a second shark headed toward her friend. Out of the corner of her eye, she saw another shark headed toward them, and then another. Soon, the RBI agents were surrounded by a whole group of sharks, circling menacingly.

"Those sharks look like they're expecting dinner," said Alek.

"What do we do?" asked Li.

"Swim for your life!" said Alek.

At that moment, a shark broke from the circle and headed toward Alek. He moved out of the way, jumping sideways quickly. He turned the speed up on his PPP and saw Kate and Li adjusting the power on their power packs too. His jetpack was much more powerful than the girls' smaller propulsion systems and he knew that he had to do something to help them.

Alek whipped through the water toward the sharks, trying to lead them away from Kate and Li. Kate dove through plants and Li sharply changed direction, both trying to lose the sharks. Li tried to hide behind some large coral, but the shark that had been following her appeared alongside, sending her darting away again.

Alek saw a narrow fissure in the rock beside him and ducked into it. It led into a small cavern, but big enough to hold three agents ...

Li was running out of options and was

beginning to get tired. She thought to herself that if she had known that she would be swimming away from hungry sharks, she would have asked Dr. Maxwell for the more powerful jetpack, like Alek's. As she felt the water around her feet stir, she dove through a gap in a rock. The shark was closing in on her. In front, another shark was headed toward her too, obviously sensing that this prey was tiring. There was no way out now. Moving as close as she could to the rock face beside her, Li closed her eyes, preparing herself for the worst.

6

Dramatic Discoveries

Just as she thought it was the end of everything, Li felt a huge tug, as if she was being pulled sideways. She was expecting it to be followed by agonizing pain as the shark's jaws clamped down around her. But the pain never came.

"Li?" for a moment she imagined that she heard her name being called. "Li!" it came again, more forcefully this time.

Slowly opening her eyes, Li found herself in

a dark cave, facing Alek. He had pulled her into the fissure in the rock at the last minute!

"Are you okay?" Alek asked.

Nodding, Li tried to steady her heart, which was beating faster than she thought possible. She saw Alek lean back out of the fissure and grab something. A moment later Kate appeared inside the small cave with them.

"Thanks, that was close," she said.

The sharks gathered outside the entrance. They could see the agents inside but they couldn't fit through the narrow gap.

"Well, we're not safe yet," Alek told her. "I don't know how we're going to get out again."

"What about the tunnel behind us?" asked Li.

The other two agents looked at her, and then shone their lights over the back wall of the cave. There really was a tunnel there that neither of them had seen.

"I can hear what sounds like a stream

somewhere, which means that this tunnel leads into somewhere with air," said Li.

"Then lead the way," said Alek.

Following the sound of the water running somewhere in the distance, the agents made their way through a twisting maze of rock tunnels. Their lights picked out small fish and moray eels that made these rocks their home.

At last, the tunnel opened out. The agents found themselves in a huge cavern. Shining their lights into the darkness, they saw

toppled ornate columns and ruined stone archways. They had found the remains of the underwater city!

"This is amazing!" cried Kate, bubbles streaming from her mask as she swam farther into the cavern. "This column must have been huge!" Kate said excitedly, as she studied a large chunk of stone that looked as if something had broken off it. "I bet if it was still standing it would be a record."

Li looked around more carefully. She was almost scared of what she was going to see. The whole cavern was underwater; she could see no surface at all. She swam very slowly, staying as close as she could to Alek, when her eyes

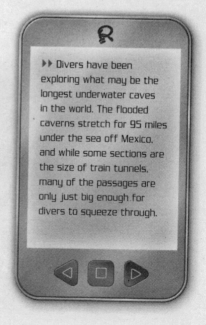

▶▶ Divers have been exploring what may be the longest underwater caves in the world. The flooded caverns stretch for 95 miles under the sea off Mexico, and while some sections are the size of train tunnels, many of the passages are only just big enough for divers to squeeze through.

finally landed on the thing she had been most terrified of.

There in front of her, stretching out of the ground as if reaching from a world beyond, was a twisted, disintegrating, and decaying hand. Li gasped and grabbed onto Alek. Now that she had seen one, everywhere she looked she could see the beckoning hands, and strangely-positioned legs. She screwed her eyes up tight, but it was no good, she still knew that they were there.

"Can you see them?" Li asked Alek. "Are they moving?"

"No they're not," said Alek. "I'm sure there's nothing to worry about." Li could feel Alek tensing though, preparing to fight, or move quickly out of the area.

"You stay here," he told her, "I'll swim over and see what they are."

Li wasn't sure whether she liked the idea of Alek swimming away, but she knew that she didn't want to get any closer to one of those

ghostly hands.

"It feels as if it's made of stone," Alek's voice came through Li's radio and she opened her eyes. "I think Kate was right about the people being covered in volcanic rock."

Kate swam over to Alek.

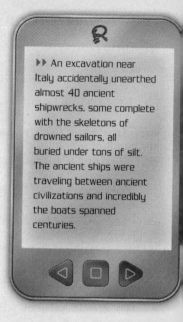

An excavation near Italy accidentally unearthed almost 40 ancient shipwrecks, some complete with the skeletons of drowned sailors, all buried under tons of silt. The ancient ships were traveling between ancient civilizations and incredibly the boats spanned centuries.

"It doesn't look like they met a very nice end," she said as bubbles rose from her diving mask. "But they are most definitely dead and have been since this particular volcano erupted, probably thousands of years ago."

"Wait, what's this?" asked Alek.

Li braced herself waiting to hear that she had been right and there was something horrible, and alive, in the middle of these ruins.

"It looks like a treasure chest," said Kate. "Li,

come and see if you recognize the art on the lid. I'm not sure about it."

Trying to be brave, Li swam over toward the other agents. She tried to look only at the chest and ignore the eerie sights around her and the ghostly hands reaching for help.

"I don't really recognize it as any sort of ancient pictogram," Li told them, trying to focus. "Maybe it's because I'm not thinking straight though," she said. "Perhaps whatever's inside will help me. Alek do you think you can open it?"

Alek strained as he tried to pry open the chest that could have been sealed shut for thousands of years. The weight of the water pressing down on the lid made it harder, but Alek's amazing strength made it look easy. It opened slowly at first, fractions of an inch at a time, until the hinges gave way and the lid sprang upward.

Inside the chest was a collection of strange

objects: a large crab with a shell shaped like a human face, the skeleton of a fish with four feet, a mummified seahorse, and a shark's tooth bigger than Alek's hand—all of which would have been perfectly at home in the halls of Ripley High!

Nestled in the middle of this unusual collection was something much more familiar.

"It's a rusted tin," said Li, bubbles rising from her mask as she pointed toward the red and yellow tin with its beautiful decoration. After finding an old artifact a little while ago, the RBI had found themselves on a quest to find other such artifacts hidden by Robert Ripley. The Ripley founder had concealed clues for them in tins all over the world, usually linked to something completely unbelievable. It looked like they had just found another clue. Alek reached in and pulled the tin out. As soon as it broke free from the chest, Li clamped her hands over her ears. Less than a second later, the whole cavern began to vibrate. There was a loud creaking sound from the enormous rock wall beside them.

"It's the curse!" shouted Li, almost in tears because she was so frightened.

A crack appeared, splitting the rock like a jagged fork of lightning. Smaller rocks broke away, falling like rain to the ground, and then a huge boulder came loose. It, too, began to fall, picking up speed as it did and heading straight toward the RBI agents.

Quaking Cavern

As the boulder continued to hurtle toward the very spot on which they were standing, Alek, Kate, and Li swam furiously to get out the way.

"What happened?" asked Alek as he moved to safety. "Did I set off a booby trap, like in one of those treasure hunter movies?"

"No, I think it's worse than that," Kate told him. The agents were having to shout now so that they could hear each other over the noise and movement of the water.

"It's the curse!" Li said again. "Like in that Egyptian tomb."

"No, I think we are on a fault line," said Kate.

"What does that mean?" asked Li.

"The Earth's crust is split into sections," Kate began. "They're called plates and they are constantly moving. A fault line is where two plates meet and, as those plates rub against each other, it can cause earthquakes or tidal waves."

"And are we on one of those fault lines?" asked Li.

"Yes, I think so," Kate dodged the head of a statue that had come loose.

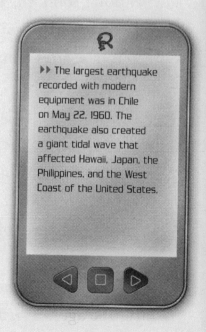

▶▶ The largest earthquake recorded with modern equipment was in Chile on May 22, 1960. The earthquake also created a giant tidal wave that affected Hawaii, Japan, the Philippines, and the West Coast of the United States.

"That would explain what happened to the city in the first place," said Alek, bubbles from his mask collecting around his face.

"If it is ancient," said Kate. "I'm not so sure. Some of the carvings I was looking at were done with laser technology. I'm fairly sure the Egyptians didn't have lasers!"

"Perhaps they really were an advanced civilization," suggested Alek.

"I don't think so," said Kate.

Before either of her colleagues could respond, a huge column near them began to sway dangerously.

"We need to get out of here," said Alek. He began to head to the other side of the cavern, hoping to find a tunnel that would lead them out, but as he swam, the broken top of an archway cut through the water toward the agents.

Alek saw the monstrous piece of stone and darted to the side, using the speed he had built

up during his Olympic training. He reached out and found Kate's arm so he pulled her with him. With his other hand, he tried to find Li, but she was too far behind. Kate and Alek could only watch from a safe distance as the arch fell on Li.

Kate tried to go to her friend, but Alek held her back until the rubble had stopped moving.

"Wait, or you'll be crushed too," he told her.

As soon as it was safe, he let her go and swam toward Li too. Alek heard Kate gasp with relief as she saw that Li was alive, but he could see that she was in trouble. Her foot was trapped under a large boulder, and the breathing tube that delivered the recycled air to her face mask was crushed, wedged tightly between two pieces of the broken stone.

Seeing that Li wasn't getting any air, Kate immediately started sharing her breathing mask with her friend, and Alek tried to free Li's breathing tube. But even with his super-strength, Alek was not able to get the column to move the slightest bit.

As he moved over to try to free Li's ankle, a strange figure pushed past him toward her. It was a man, covered in scars. Kate and Li looked shocked. Alek felt uneasy about the man, and

wasn't sure whether to let him near Li. The new arrival worked quickly, trying to free Li's breathing tube. Alek saw that the scars looked like they were from shark bites. The man's whole upper body was huge, and there was something odd and worrying about his hands that Alek couldn't quite make out through the water, which was now murky and clouded with debris.

The man worked on the boulder trapping Li, using all his strength to lift it, while Kate eased Li's foot from under it. Li looked petrified as the man worked. Alek knew that in her mind this would be linked to the bodies and the curse she was so sure they had activated.

▶▶ There is a condition affecting the feet that gives the impression of "webbed toes." Although it is normal for animals such as birds to have webbed feet, it is not common in humans. One in every 2,500 people are born with the condition, known as syndactyly.

At this point, the scarred man gave up trying to free Li's trapped breathing mask. Instead, he pulled her away from the column, holding on to her as he began swimming up toward the top of the cavern.

Kate and Alek both followed. As they rose through the water, Alek noticed the man's feet. There was skin between his toes that made it look as if his feet were webbed. Then he remembered that the man's hands had seemed strange too. There had been extra skin between his fingers as well!

The idea of someone with webbed hands and feet swimming off with his friend panicked Alek and he sped up. The man he was chasing was swimming as fast as a dolphin, but Alek adjusted his jet pack to its top setting. He was desperate to catch the man and find out where he was taking Li.

8

Dazzling Underwater Leisure

Eventually, Alek's head broke the surface; there was a pocket of air at the top of the cavern. He looked around and saw Li already there, gasping to catch her breath.

"Are you okay now?" the man was asking her. He spoke good English, but with a Greek accent.

"Thank you," Li spluttered between gulps of air. Her fear began to fade as she realized what this man had done for her. "You saved my life."

"What were you doing in the cavern?" the man asked. "How did you find it?"

Kate explained that they were looking for the ancient underwater city.

"Although we don't think that it's ancient at all," she said.

"Well, parts of it are about five years old," said the man.

The RBI agents looked very confused.

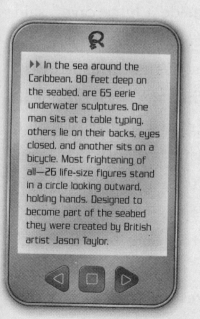

▶▶ In the sea around the Caribbean, 80 feet deep on the seabed, are 65 eerie underwater sculptures. One man sits at a table typing, others lie on their backs, eyes closed, and another sits on a bicycle. Most frightening of all—26 life-size figures stand in a circle looking outward, holding hands. Designed to become part of the seabed they were created by British artist Jason Taylor.

"I built the ruins," he explained, and then introduced himself. The man's name was Nikos Katomeri and he was a sculptor who made artworks to be displayed underwater. He had been asked to create the ocean-floor city as part of a tourist attraction.

"So they are not the remains of people who were killed horribly?" asked Li

"No, a company called Dazzling Underwater Leisure asked me to build a ruined city that tourists could explore when they came to Crete," said Nikos.

Li felt relief wash over her. She had been worrying about nothing.

"But it's hidden inside a huge cave," said Alek. "How will the tourists ever find it?"

"It's hidden because it's not finished yet," explained Nikos. "When my work is done, a big entrance will be created so that everyone will know that it's there. But until that time, my Atlantis is meant to be a big secret. That is why I was so surprised to see you three there."

"We only found the cave by accident," said Kate.

"We were trying to escape from a shark and

we got stuck in a maze of tunnels that brought us out here," said Alek.

"I've noticed a lot of shark activity in the area," said Nikos. "I think of them as my security system. They make sure that divers don't stumble upon Atlantis before it's finished. I sometimes wonder if they work for Dazzling Underwater Leisure!"

"So how do we get out?" asked Li.

"The water should be clear now," he told her. "The earthquake will have scared the sharks away. If we leave right away, you should be fine."

"I'm not sure I can remember the way through all those tunnels again," said Alek.

"That's alright, I'll come with you," said Nikos.

Kate swam over to Li. "Is your ankle okay to swim?" she asked.

"It hurts a lot," said Li. "But I think I'd rather get out of here before we look at it. I can still swim, and at least I don't have to put any weight on it."

"Okay," said Kate. "You don't have your breathing mask though. You can share mine."

"You should share with me," said Alek. "Part of my swimming training is to hold my breath for long periods of time. It's a really long way and you might need the oxygen."

Alek gave Li his diving mask and followed Nikos out of the cave into the tunnels. He noticed that Nikos didn't have a breathing mask of his own.

Nikos led them through a different series of tunnels from the ones they had taken earlier, and this new way seemed even longer. At times, Alek found his lungs straining for air as he shared his mask with Li. When they finally broke the surface of the water, the sun had set and the sky was clear. The others had surfaced before them and Kate was shining her diver's light over the dark water.

"The car's just over there," she said.

Alek turned to Nikos. "Did you swim all that way without oxygen?" he asked.

Nikos nodded. "I can hold my breath for up to 25 minutes underwater," he told them.

"That's amazing," said Kate.

"Is it?" asked Nikos. "I've never really thought about it. It's just something I can do."

He explained to the agents that he had worked underwater for a long time. Over the years, he gradually increased the length of time he was able to stay under without needing to come up for air.

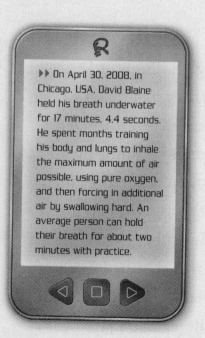

▶▶ On April 30, 2008, in Chicago, USA, David Blaine held his breath underwater for 17 minutes, 4.4 seconds. He spent months training his body and lungs to inhale the maximum amount of air possible, using pure oxygen, and then forcing in additional air by swallowing hard. An average person can hold their breath for about two minutes with practice.

"It's so much easier to see what I am doing without the bubbles that come with scuba gear," he explained.

Alek thought about the man's incredibly large upper body.

"Your lungs must have gotten a lot bigger," he said.

"My whole body seems to have adapted over time," said Nikos. He held up one of his hands, with its unusual webbing between the fingers. "I was born with this strange webbing between my fingers and toes, so the water just seemed a natural path for me to take. However, over time I have found that I can swim much faster than I used to, and I find it much easier to stay deep down in the water without the need for weights."

"That's unbelievable," said Kate. "We're from the RBI and we'd love to interview you for our database."

Nikos looked curious and started to reply, but his answer was lost as a piercing shriek drowned it out.

Kate and Alek turned to look at Li, who had

screamed. She was pointing to a spot not far from them, where a tall, sleek object was slicing through the water with alarming speed.

"Sh-shark!" she stuttered as the silver-gray dorsal fin shone in the moonlight.

9

Shark Scare

"Swim to the car as fast as you can," Alek told the others, as a second fin appeared beside him. "We'll be safe inside."

As he reached Jaws, Alek opened the door and pulled himself inside. Nikos and Li appeared next to him and climbed into the back seat.

"Where's Kate?" asked Alek.

"She was right behind me," said Li, panic

creeping into her voice. "K-a-te!" she called out into the darkness.

"There she is," said Alek as he saw Kate's diver's light bobbing a little distance from the car.

The light picked out Kate's face. She didn't normally scare easily, but now she looked

terrified. Alek shone a flashlight toward her and saw why: she was surrounded by shark fins. Immediately, Alek readied himself to jump back out of the car, but Nikos stopped him.

"If you go, then you'll both need rescuing," he said. "You stay here with Li. I'll go get Kate. I know these waters well and I'm used to dealing

with sharks."

Before Alek could object, Nikos dove into the shadowy water and disappeared beneath the waves.

For seconds that felt like hours, Kate floated there, trying not to move or disturb the water, hoping not to

▶▶ Sharks have an extra sense, courtesy of ampullae of Lorenzini, special organs that allow them to detect electromagnetic fields. Whenever a living creature moves, it creates an electromagnetic field and great white sharks are so sensitive that they can detect a minute electrical charge in the water.

attract the sharks. Then there was movement. The sharks seemed to sense something as they began to close in on Kate. Alek and Li watched as she panicked, and then a sharp tug pulled her beneath the water.

"No!" cried Alek. Li screamed as she saw her best friend go under.

Alek looked out over the sea, not quite believing what he had just seen. The sharks seemed to be moving again. They broke their circle and seemed to be headed toward Jaws.

"Close the doors!" shouted Li, as she saw the fins make a line toward them. "Quickly!"

"Wait!" a voice cried out. Nikos's head appeared. He was dragging something behind him. It was Kate, and she was alive. It was Nikos that had pulled her under the water to get her away from the sharks.

Alek pulled Kate into the car as Nikos struggled up beside her. Li grabbed a blanket and wrapped it around her friend, who looked pale from shock, as Alek hurried to close the doors. The driver's door whirred and lowered back into position just as a loud thud sounded, and the car shook.

Looking out the window, Alek saw that a hammerhead shark had charged at the car and knocked its snout as Jaws's door had closed.

"That was close," he said, as he switched on the anti-shark technology and plunged the car deeper into the sea.

"Listen," said Li. "What's that?"

The others stayed quiet, but it was a little while before what Li's hearing had picked up was clear to them.

"It sounds like a boat motor," said Kate, dropping the blanket and moving to get a better look out of the windshield.

The shape of a small boat appeared on the surface of the water above them.

"It looks like that boat from last night," said Alek, as he dimmed the headlights to help hide Jaws.

There was a splash as something was dropped into the water. It sank, hitting the car's windshield and leaving a grisly mess.

"That looks like blood," said Li, her fear returning.

The thing rolled off the hood and into the beam of the headlights.

"It's a large piece of meat," said Alek.

"It's not a body part, is it?" asked Li quickly.

"No, I'd say it's beef," Alek assured her.

A shark swooped past and grabbed the meat. A second shark tried to fight for it, until another piece drifted down from the boat and the shark pounced on that instead.

"I think whoever is in that boat is feeding the sharks," said Nikos.

"Maybe you were right, and the company that hired you is trying to bring sharks into the area to scare divers away," suggested Alek.

"That sounds more like something DUL would do," said Li.

"Wait a minute!" said Kate, as something clicked in her mind. She was still shaken from her close call with the sharks, but her amazing memory and reasoning powers seemed to even work well when she wasn't feeling her best. "Nikos, what did you say that company was called?"

"Their name is Dazzling Underwater Leisure," he told her.

"Dazzling—Underwater—Leisure," Kate repeated slowly. "The company's initials are D–U–L."

Looking up, the agents saw that there were now three boats in the water above them. One of the boats had an all too familiar logo on the bottom of its hull.

"That's a DUL boat alright," said Alek.

"If you move a bit closer, I can hear what they're saying," offered Li.

Alek drove Jaws toward the DUL boats so that Li's amazing hearing could filter out the noise of the boats and pick up the DUL agents' conversation. The sharks moved away, put off by the anti-shark technology.

"The DUL agents are confused," Li told them. "They can't understand why the sharks are moving away from the meat and not going toward it."

Lights flashed in the water around them.

"They've seen us," Li explained. "They think

we're some sort of giant shark and they seem quite scared." She laughed at the DUL agents' confusion.

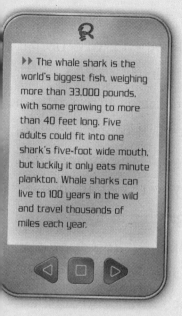

▶▶ The whale shark is the world's biggest fish, weighing more than 33,000 pounds, with some growing to more than 40 feet long. Five adults could fit into one shark's five-foot wide mouth, but luckily it only eats minute plankton. Whale sharks can live to 100 years in the wild and travel thousands of miles each year.

"That gives me an idea," said Alek.

He cut Jaws's engine and let the car glide silently upward. The periscope tower broke the surface, but Alek kept the rest of the car under the water. To anyone above the surface it would look like a large dorsal fin. Alek gently edged the car forward toward the DUL boats.

"Shark! Great, big, giant shark!"

The RBI agents didn't need Li to tell them what the men in the boats were shouting. It was loud enough to hear now. They watched the commotion on a screen that transmitted the view from the periscope. It was utter chaos above them.

The DUL agents were desperately trying to get away. All three boats leaped into action at once, with everyone on them in a blind panic. The boats drove in crazed circles as the drivers shouted instructions at each other. Only no one was listening to what the other DUL drivers were saying. They were just all focused on getting away—and getting away fast! The DUL boats were all doing incredible speeds as they attempted their escape. As a result, two of the boats ran toward each other and crashed, sending the DUL agents on board scrambling for life rafts. The third boat, however, was luckier. It picked a safer path and missed the other two boats.

Alek plunged the car back under the water and speeded up to overtake the remaining DUL boat. He timed it carefully, bringing Jaws up so that the periscope lifted the escaping DUL boat right out of the water!

For a second, the boat was balanced in mid-air; then it wobbled and toppled back into the sea.

The RBI agents watched as the DUL agents swam furiously toward the life rafts, shouting at their friends to come and save them. But the

agents in the lifeboats were paddling as hard as they could, away from their colleagues—and the giant shark.

Megalodon

When they arrived back on shore, Kate interviewed Nikos, getting all the information they would need for his entry in the Ripley's database.

"So what did this DUL want me for?" he asked.

"They did want you to create an underwater city," Kate told him. "But they weren't doing it to attract tourists! DUL wanted to leak the location of the ruins once you had finished, hoping that we would be fooled into entering it into the database as a real archaeological discovery!"

"And you were right," said Alek. "They really were trying to attract sharks. They couldn't risk anyone finding the city until they were ready."

▶▶ A shark's sense of smell is so sensitive that it can smell a drop of blood from a quarter of a mile away. Some can detect a single chemical molecule among one million others using their noses; this is like finding a golf ball in Loch Ness. Scientists have discovered that 14 percent of the great white shark's brain is devoted purely to smell.

Nikos sat down with his head in his hands. "I have been such a fool," he said. "I only wanted to help bring more tourists to my island. Now all my hard work has been for nothing!"

"I think we can help you out there," said Alek. "Why don't you finish Atlantis and then open it as a tourist attraction yourself?"

Nikos looked up, interested in Alek's idea.

"We know the man who runs the Poseidon Diving School," said Kate. "I'm sure he'd be thrilled to have some underwater ruins for his diving groups to explore. Even if they are not really ancient."

Li appeared beside them. She had been looking for something in the car since they brought Jaws ashore.

"Found it," she said, holding the thing she had been searching for out in front of her. It was the tin from the treasure chest.

"Where did you get this from?" Alek asked Nikos.

"It was my father's," said Nikos, taking the tin. He turned it over in his hands as he spoke. "Atlantis was his idea. He died a few years ago and in his things I found the plans for an underwater city. The tin was his, too. It had a note on it signed "an old friend," asking that the tin be hidden among the ruins when they were finally built. It was when I first started looking around to see if there was any interest in anything like this that Dazzling Underwater Leisure contacted me."

He tried to open the tin, but it was stuck fast after being shut for so many years. Alek took it and tried to pry it open. His face went red with the effort, but eventually the lid popped off and something flew out of it. Li caught it carefully

and examined it. It was a small whale carved from shell. She turned it over and gasped as she saw the marking on the bottom. A small "RR" had been carved into it.

"They're Rip's initials," she said.

"It looks a bit like his signature," said Kate. "Rip must have been the friend who asked for the tin to be put in the ruins!"

"It wouldn't surprise me if Rip had left that tin," said Alek, once the three agents were in Jaws and heading back to Bion Island. "He's been behind all the other tins we've found."

"I just wonder what they all mean," said Kate, as her R-phone began to buzz. She pulled it out of her pocket and saw that it was Mr. Cain. Quickly, she put it on speakerphone and answered it.

"Are you all there?" Mr. Cain asked. All three agents said hello to their teacher.

"Well done on the Atlantis mission," he told

them. "But while you are there, I have another mystery for you to look into."

The agents sat quietly waiting for their new brief.

"We've had quite a few reports over the last 24 hours from the area you are in. People have been sighting a giant shark that they think might be a prehistoric megalodon."

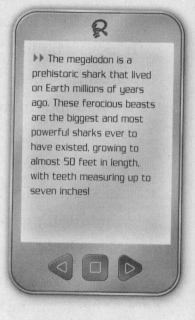

▶▶ The megalodon is a prehistoric shark that lived on Earth millions of years ago. These ferocious beasts are the biggest and most powerful sharks ever to have existed, growing to almost 50 feet in length, with teeth measuring up to seven inches!

"I think it might be Jaws, Sir," said Alek.

"No, no, the reports definitely say it's a shark," said Mr. Cain.

The agents looked at each other and smiled. Dr. Maxwell had some explaining to do about his new car!

RIPLEY'S DATABASE ENTRY

RIPLEY FILE NUMBER : 54763

MISSION BRIEF : Believe it or not, an underwater graveyard has been discovered near Crete, Greece. Investigate accuracy of these accounts for Ripley database.

CODE NAME : Undersea Sculptor

REAL NAME : Nikos Katomeri

LOCATION : Crete, Greece

AGE : 39

HEIGHT : 5ft 10 in

WEIGHT : 11 st

VIDEO CAPTURE

UNUSUAL CHARACTERISTICS :

Incredibly large upper body due to expanded lung capacity, webbed feet, webbing between fingers. Covered in scars from previous battles with sharks and other sea creatures. Ability to hold breath for up to 25 minutes underwater.

RBI DATABASE **APPROVED!**

INVESTIGATING AGENTS :

Alek Filipov, Kate Jones, Li Yong

 YOUR NEXT ASSIGNMENT

WINGS OF FEAR

Prologue

It was almost 9:30 and Abby was going to be late for work – again! She rushed out of the underground station, taking the steps up to street level two at a time. Abby had tried so hard to be on time, but last night she had had dinner with her best friend Clare, who she hadn't seen for ages, and they had talked for hours. Then, when her alarm went off this morning, she had just been *so* tired!

As she rushed along the pavement, Abby tried to work out how she was going to get everything done before the Ripley's museum, where she worked, opened – in half an hour.

Suddenly, Abby heard a strange noise. She pulled her phone out of her pocket to see if someone was calling. It wasn't the noise her phone normally made, but it would be just like Clare to have changed the ringtone while she wasn't looking. But the noise wasn't her phone. It grew louder and louder – a high-pitched whine, like an airplane makes just before its engines kick in. Abby looked up to see if there was a plane in trouble, shielding her eyes from the morning sun. As she did so, a large shadow appeared. Huge wings blocked out the sun, and warmth like a fire swallowed up the cool morning breeze. Bright flames lit up the sky as a large flying creature shot past above Abby's head.

Thinking quickly, she switched her phone

to camera mode and tried to get some film of the strange thing. Nobody would believe her about this unless they saw it! Running down the street she filmed until the *thing*, whatever it was, disappeared from view.

Replaying the video Abby looked closely at the screen. It almost seemed as if the creature was surrounded by fire. Abby felt herself go cold with fear. What could it possibly have been?

Closing her phone, Abby ran the rest of the way to work – terrified that the creature might return.

ENTER THE STRANGE WORLD OF RIPLEY'S...

▶▶ Believe it or not, there is a lot of truth in this remarkable tale. The Ripley's team travels the globe to track down true stories that will amaze you. Read on to find out about real Ripley's case files and discover incredible facts about some of the extraordinary people and places in our world.

Ripley's
Believe It or Not!

▶▶ FREEDIVING

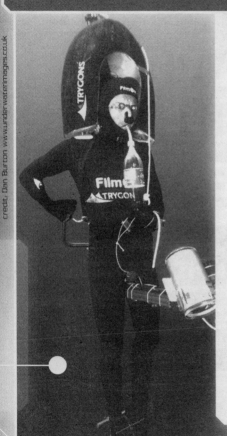

credit: Dan Burton www.underwaterimages.co.uk

Champion freediver Herbert Nitsch, plunged to an incredible depth of 702 feet with no breathing apparatus in 2008. The dive took 4 minutes 24 seconds.

▶▶ With no scuba gear, the lungs of freedivers can shrink to the size of a fist as they pass 100 feet.

▶▶ A diver's heart rate can drop below 20 beats per minute.

▶▶ Freedivers are at risk when their brains become starved of oxygen.

▶▶ Top female diver Tanya Streeter, from the British Virgin Islands, dove down over 525 feet in the Turks and Caicos islands in 2002. She can hold her breath for six minutes.

FRANCE

ITALY

Black Sea

SPAIN

GREECE

TURKEY

THIRA

MOROCCO

TUNISIA

CRETE

CYPRUS

ALGERIA

Sahara Desert

LIBYA

EGYPT

▶▶ Some experts think that an ancient volcanic eruption 3000 years ago on the island of Thira in the Mediterranean inspired the story of Atlantis. The eruption would have destroyed whole cities, causing tsunamis and clouds of dust an incredible 50 miles high.

▶▶ The lost city of Atlantis was first described over 2000 years ago in the writings of ancient Greek writer Plato as an island destroyed by the sea.

▶ In 2004, a US researcher claimed to have discovered the real Atlantis to the south of Cyprus, buried over 11,000 years ago by a great flood.

▶ Over time, the advance of the Sahara Desert toward the Mediterranean Sea has buried some 600 cities.

▶▶ Giulia Ferdinanda, a tiny volcanic island off the coast of Italy, regularly emerges from, and disappears under, the waves of the Mediterranean Sea.

▶▶ The biggest flood ever occurred about 7,500 years ago when water poured over a narrow lowland to the east of the Mediterranean, creating the Black Sea. This torrent drowned towns, villages, and farms.

CASE FILE #002

▶▶ Italian Livio de Marchi created a full-size Ferrari replica car entirely from wood and floated it down the canals of Venice.

▶▶ SQUBA CAR

credit: Rinspeed

Swiss auto company, Rinspeed, has actually created a sports car that operates underwater.

▶▶ The sQuba automobile transforms into a diving vehicle at the touch of a button.

▶▶ The car is capable of diving to a depth of 33 feet.

▶▶ The sQuba was inspired by an amphibious Lotus car that appeared in a James Bond film.

▶▶ Sharks don't have any bones. Their bodies are supported by muscle and dense cartilage, much like our own ears and noses.

▶▶ Sharks evolved over 350 million years ago—long before dinosaurs walked the Earth.

credit: ©francois brisson—fotolia.com

SHARKS

▶▶ The megamouth shark is 16 feet long and weighs 2000 pounds, but this shark only feeds on tiny creatures hundreds of feet down. Only 44 have ever been seen.

▶▶ Tiger sharks have been cut open to reveal fuel cans, bicycle tires, lumps of wood, parts of a dead dog, and tin drums.

▶▶ Sharks live in every ocean of the world and they can even be found in rivers.

▶▶ Some types of shark in the open sea have to keep moving, otherwise they will suffocate.

▶▶ The shark is the only fish that can blink its eyes.

123

▶▶ WATERY GRAVES

A cemetery has been built under the sea, three miles off the coast of Florida, with bronze lions, roads, walls, and city gates, designed as the ultimate resting place for those who love the sea.

▶▶ The memorial reef has enough room for the remains of 125,000 people.

▶▶ The cemetery covers 16 acres of the seabed.

▶▶ The cemetery is a recreation of a lost city and the world's largest man-made reef.

▶▶ The graves are intended to become a haven for sea creatures and human divers in life and deat

▶▶ RIPLEY

▶▶ In his lifetime, Ripley traveled over 450,000 miles looking for oddities—the distance from Earth to the Moon and back again.

▶▶ Ripley had a large collection of cars, but he couldn't drive. He also bought a Chinese sailing boat, called Mon Lei, but he couldn't swim.

▶▶ Ripley was so popular that his weekly mailbag often exceeded 170,000 letters, all full of weird and wacky suggestions for his cartoon strip.

▶▶ He kept a 20-foot-long boa constrictor as a pet in his New York home.

▶▶ Ripley's Believe It or Not! cartoon is the longest-running cartoon strip in the world, read in 42 countries and 17 languages every day.

In 1918, Robert Ripley became fascinated by strange facts while he was working as a cartoonist at the *New York Globe*. He was passionate about travel and, by 1940, had visited no less than 201 countries, gathering artifacts and searching for stories that would be right for his column, which he named Believe It or Not!

Ripley bought an island estate at Mamaroneck, New York, and filled the huge house there with unusual objects and odd creatures that he'd collected on his explorations.

PACKED WITH FUN & GAMES, THE **RBI** WEBSITE IS HERE! CHECK IT OUT

REVIEWS

DOWNLOADS

MAPS & DATA

MORE TEAM TAL

FUN!

THE NEXT FILES